MY GRAMMY SHAKES. DOES YOURS?

by SUZANNE MASSO

illustrations by DAWN SALVATERRA

Published by BookBaby Publishing,
7905 N. Crescent Blvd. Pennsauken, N.J.

ISBN: 978-1-09834-501-3

This book is dedicated to the heart and soul of my life - my grandchildren, Claire and Michael. They give me joy simply by being!

Acknowledgement and special thanks to my family and friends for their constant support and encouragement in writing this book and in my PD journey. A debt of gratitude to my PD family at Rock Steady Boxing - the coaches, volunteers and participants for their ongoing inspiration and motivation. Lastly thanks to my talented illustrator, Dawn who made my words and ideas come alive through her illustrations.

Hi! My name is Claire and I am six years old.
This is my brother Michael, and he is four years old.

We live with our mom and dad like most kids.

We also have grandparents like a lot of kids.
We have four—Nana, Pops, Grammy, and Grampy.

They do NOT live with us, but they visit us and we like to visit them.

This story is about my Grammy. She's the one who shakes. This means that sometimes her hand and arm shake even when she doesn't want them to. The special word for that is a tremor

Grammy has a special sickness called PD. The fancy name is Parkinson's Disease..
Grammy says a lot of people have it, but she's the only one Michael and I know

My grampy likes to tease her and says, "Grammy makes the best milkshakes!"
Grammy always laughs, but I think sometimes it hurts her feelings.

Sometimes Grammy has trouble getting up from playing with Michael and me.
That's okay because we're strong and we can help her get up.

Grammy doesn't always walk very speedy, but it's speedy enough to take us to the park and that's just fine with us.

Grammy speaks kind of quiet sometimes, and when that happens,
we pretend it's "Shout it Out" time. That's a game we play where we're all
allowed to use our outside voices inside. It's a lot of fun, but very noisy.

Grammy can do lots of things that maybe your grammy
(or Nana or Gigi or Grandma does).

She bakes yummy cookies. Does yours?

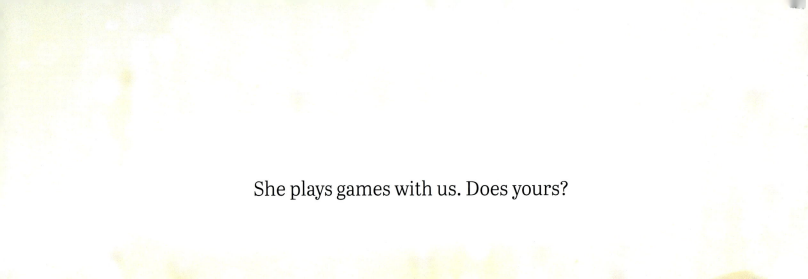

She plays games with us. Does yours?

She makes our favorite food when we visit. Does yours?

She reads to us and snuggles. Does yours?

She takes us for ice cream. Does yours?

She gives us lots of hugs and kisses. Does yours?

Our grammy also does something I bet your grammy doesn't.
She boxes with real boxing gloves. Does yours?

Grammy boxes to stay strong and she says it's her way to fight Parkinson's.
It makes her "rock steady."

She even let Michael and me try on her boxing gloves. I felt so STRONG!

Maybe that's how Grammy feels when she's wearing them. I hope so!

Well, our Grammy shakes, but we love her very much.

Perhaps your Grammy or Grampy shakes too, or forgets things, or can't breathe well, or needs to use a cane, or takes a lot of naps.

It really doesn't matter, because they still love you and ...you should love them anyway.

Michael and I do! Do you?